STUFFED WITH LOVE

Hylas Publishing
129 Main Street
Irvington, New York 10533
www.hylaspublishing.com

Hylas Publishing
Editorial Director: Lori Baird
Art Directors: Edwin Kuo, Gus Yoo
Production Coordinator: Sarah Reilly

Project Credits
Editor: Sarah Reilly
Managing Editor: Myrsini Stephanides
Designer: Shani Parsons

ISBN: 1-59258-134-X

Library of Congress Cataloging-in-Publication Data
available upon request.

Printed and bound in Italy
Distributed by National Book Network

First American Edition published in 2005

10   9   8   7   6   5   4   3   2   1

STUFFED WiTH LOVE

HYLAS

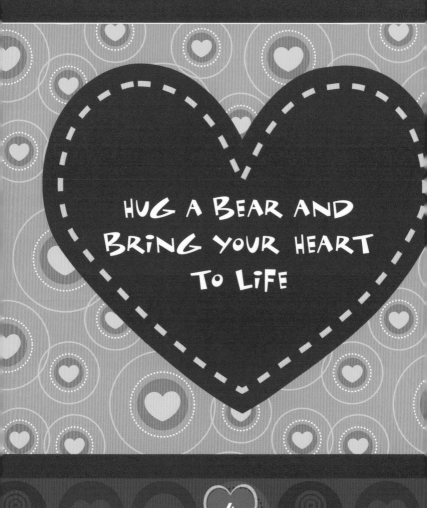

HUG A BEAR AND
BRING YOUR HEART
TO LIFE

i LOVE YOU

5

BEARS GUARD
YOUR HEART
IN THEIR
PAWS

NO MATTER HOW YOU'RE STUFFED, THERE'S ALWAYS ROOM FOR LOVE

BEARS LIVE BY
THE RULES
OF THE HEART

iT'S BETTER TO HAVE
LOVED A BEAR
AND LOST iT, THAN
NEVER TO HAVE
LOVED iT
AT ALL

14

THE FUR MAY FADE,
BUT THE LOVE
LASTS FUR·EVER

NOTHING IS MORE POWERFUL THAN THE PAWSITIVE POWER OF LOVE

18

TOGETHER FUR·EVER,
NEVER APART.
MAYBE
IN DISTANCE,
BUT NEVER
AT HEART.

FRIENDS BRING
OUT THE BEST
IN YOU

21

LOVE iS
PAWSiTiVELY
PRECiOUS

WHEN iT'S DARK,
LET THE LovE
in youR HEART
LiGHT THE
WaY

A SMILE
IS A WINDOW
INTO YOUR
HEART

BEARS ARE MEASURED BY THE SIZE OF THEIR HEART

30

OPEN YOUR PAWS TO LOVE

WHERE BEST FRIENDS ARE MADE®

OTHER BOOKS FROM HYLAS PUBLISHING IN
THE BUILD·A·BEAR WORKSHOP® SERIES:

CELE·BEAR·ATE!

FRIENDS FUR LIFE

PAWSITIVE THOUGHTS

BUILD·A·BEAR WORKSHOP®
FURRY FRIENDS HALL OF FAME
THE OFFICIAL COLLECTOR'S GUIDE

Hylas Publishing would like to thank Ginger Bandoni,
Melissa Segal, Lori Zelkind, and Patty Sullivan at
Evergreen Concepts. Many thanks to Laura Kurzu, Mindy
Barsky, and of course, C.E.B. Maxine Clark.